I KNOW OPPOSITES

SOFT AND HARD

by Gini Holland

Reading consultant: Susan Nations, M.Ed., author/literacy coach/
consultant in literacy development

WEEKLY READER
PUBLISHING

Please visit our web site at: www.garethstevens.com
For a free color catalog describing our list of high-quality books,
call 1-800-542-2595 (USA) or 1-800-387-3178 (Canada).

Library of Congress Cataloging-in-Publication Data

Holland, Gini.
    Soft and hard / Gini Holland.
      p. cm. — (I know opposites)
    ISBN: 978-0-8368-8296-4 (lib. bdg.)
    ISBN: 978-0-8368-8301-5 (softcover)
    1. Hardness—Juvenile literature. I. Title.
TA418.42.H65   2007
620.1'126—dc22   2007006688

This edition first published in 2008 by
Weekly Reader® Books
An imprint of Gareth Stevens Publishing
1 Reader's Digest Road
Pleasantville, NY 10570-7000 USA

Managing editor: Valerie J. Weber
Art direction: Tammy West
Graphic designer: David Kowalski
Photo researcher: Diane Laska-Swanke
Production: Jessica Yanke

Picture credits: Cover (left), title page (left), pp. 6, 8, 13, 14, 15, 16 (upper
right) © Diane Laska-Swanke; cover (right), title page (right), p. 7 © EyeWire;
pp. 4, 9, 16 (upper left and lower left) © David Young-Wolff/PhotoEdit; p. 5
© Spencer Grant/PhotoEdit; p. 10 © Corel; p. 11 © Felicia Martinez/PhotoEdit;
pp. 12, 16 (lower right) © Chris Collins/CORBIS

Printed in the United States of America

1 2 3 4 5 6 7 8 9 11 10 09 08 07

Note to Educators and Parents

Reading is such an exciting adventure for young children! They are beginning to integrate their oral language skills with written language. To encourage children along the path to early literacy, books must be colorful, engaging, and interesting; they should invite the young reader to explore both the print and the pictures.

I Know Opposites is a series designed to help children read and learn about the key concept of opposites. In this series, young readers learn what makes things opposite each other by exploring familiar, fun examples of things that are *Alive and Not Alive*, *Soft and Hard*, *Light and Heavy*, and *Hot and Cold*.

Each book is specially designed to support the young reader in the reading process. The familiar topics are appealing to young children and invite them to read — and re-read — again and again. The full-color photographs and enhanced text further support the student during the reading process.

In addition to serving as wonderful picture books in schools, libraries, homes, and other places where children learn to love reading, these books are specifically intended to be read within an instructional guided reading group. This small group setting allows beginning readers to work with a fluent adult model as they make meaning from the text. After children develop fluency with the text and content, the book can be read independently. Children and adults alike will find these books supportive, engaging, and fun!

— Susan Nations, M.Ed., author, literacy coach, and consultant in literacy development

The yarn is soft.

The ball is hard.

The hat is soft.

The helmet is hard.

The toy is soft.

The bat is hard.

The rabbit is soft.

The shell is hard.

The chick is soft.

The egg is hard.

The pillow is soft.

The table is hard.

15

Which are soft?

Which are hard?